This book belongs to:

....

....

....

For Lily, with love

A BRUBAKER, FORD & FRIENDS BOOK,
an imprint of The Templar Company Limited

First published in the UK in hardback in 2011 by Templar Publishing
This softback edition published in 2012 by Templar Publishing,
The Granary, North Street, Dorking, Surrey, RH4 1DN, UK
www.templarco.co.uk

Text copyright © 2011 Bryan Forbes Ltd.
Illustration copyright © 2011 Emma Chichester Clark

First softback edition

ISBN 978-1-84877-543-5

Printed in China

What Will You Be, Grandma?

Nanette Newman

illustrated by
Emma Chichester Clark

B∥F∥&∥F

BRUBAKER, FORD & FRIENDS

AN IMPRINT OF THE TEMPLAR COMPANY LIMITED

One day Lily asked her grandma,

"What do you think you'll be
when you grow up?"

"Well," said her grandma,
"a lot of people think I've
grown up already."

"Oh no," said Lily, "you've
got a long way to go yet."

"I wonder what I could be?"
said her grandma.

"You could be a lady who goes to schools and says, 'No more lessons today, everyone go off and play,'" said Lily.

"Good idea," said her grandma.

"Or," said Lily, "you could grow
wings and fly around the world,
making sure people were kind
to their cats and dogs like me."

"I'd like to have wings,"
said her grandma.

"So would I," said Lily.

"Or you could become an artist and
paint rainbows on children's faces."

"And butterflies," said grandma.

"And tigers," said Lily.

"What fun," said her grandma.

"Or you could become a special doctor and
when somebody fell over, you could give
them your magic kiss and they'd feel better."

Lily's grandma nodded.
"Just like I did for you yesterday."

"Exactly," said Lily.

"Or you could become a gardener and grow
flowers that never die – people would like that."

"They would," said her grandma.
"I could also grow Brussels sprouts
that taste like strawberry ice cream."

"And cabbage that tastes like
chocolate cake," said Lily.

"Delicious!" said her grandma.

"Or maybe, at weekends," said Lily, "you could be a lady who makes lollipops and gives them away free, so that children can save their pocket money."

"I think your friends would like that," said her grandma.

"They would," said Lily.

"Or you could be an entertainer who goes to birthday parties and makes sure everybody gets a balloon and presents that are really good."

"Could I go in fancy dress?" asked her grandma.

"Definitely," said Lily.

"Or, you could grow up to be
a fairy with a magic wand who
stops rooms getting untidy."

"I could," said her grandma,
"but perhaps I'm too old
to be a fairy."

"No, you're not. Old fairies
are the best," said Lily.

"Let me think," said Lily.
"You could do children's homework
for them so that their teachers
always give them a star."

"I'm glad you think I'm that clever,"
said her grandma.

"You are," said Lily.

They thought for a bit while Lily put on her pyjamas and her grandma found her favourite bear.

"I know what I'd like to be," said her grandma. "I'd like to be a lady with a little granddaughter called Lily who she loved up to the sky and down again."

She tucked Lily up in bed
and gave her a goodnight kiss.

"Yes," said Lily, sleepily,
"I think you'd be very
good at that."